WELCOME TO THE WORLD
OF
Geronimo Stilton

Published by Sweet Cherry Publishing Limited
Unit 36, Vulcan House,
Vulcan Road,
Leicester, LE5 3EF,
United Kingdom

First published in the UK in 2018
2019 edition

2 4 6 8 10 9 7 5 3

ISBN: 978-1-78226-375-3

Text by Geronimo Stilton
Art Director: Iacopo Bruno
Graphic Designer: Laura Dal Maso / theWorldofDOT
Original cover illustration by Roberto Ronchi and Alessandro Muscillo
Concept of illustration by Roberta Bianchi, produced by Giuseppe Ferrario and Flavio Fausone
with assistance from Elisabetta Natella
Initial and final page illustrations by Roberto Ronchi and Ennio Bufi MAD5, Studio Parlapà and
Andrea Cavallini. Map illustrations by Andrea Da Rold and Andrea Cavallini
Cover layout and typography by Elena Distefano
Interior layout and typography by Rhiannon Izard, Kellie Jones, Chris Ogle and Amy Wong
Graphics by Paolo Zadra
© 2013 Edizioni Piemme S.p.A., Palazzo Mondadori – Via Mondadori, 1 – 20090 Segrate
© 2018 English edition, Sweet Cherry Publishing
International Rights © Atlantyca S.p.A. – Via Leopardi 8, 20123 Milano, Italy
Translation © 2015, Atlantyca S.p.A.

Original title: *Il tesoro di Rapa Nui*
Based on an original idea by Elisabetta Dami

www.geronimostilton.com/uk

www.sweetcherrypublishing.com

Printed and bound in India
I.IPP001

Geronimo Stilton

THE TREASURE OF EASTER ISLAND

Sweet Cherry

PUBLISHING

An Adventure to Remember!

I'm ready to tell you about an incredible adventure I'll never forget. This story is very special to me because it takes place in one of the most **mysterious** places on Earth ...

The whole thing started on a beautiful spring morning. Oops! What terrible manners! I haven't introduced myself yet. My name is Stilton, *Geronimo*

Stilton, and I'm the publisher of The Rodent's Gazette, the most famous newspaper on Mouse Island.

Anyway, that spring morning I was hard at work in my office. (For the record, I'm always hard at work when I'm in the office, even if my grandfather William Shortpaws says otherwise!) I was with Susie Shuttermouse, our new staff photographer. We were deciding which photo to put on the front page of our next issue. Susie is also best friends with my sister Thea. And Thea is the newspaper's special correspondent.

Susie pointed to a photo of the **AMAZON RAINFOREST**. The image showed a crew of rats chopping down trees and vegetation.

AMAZON RAiNFOREST

SUSIE SHUTTERMOUSE

Susie Shuttermouse is *The Rodent's Gazette*'s official photographer and Thea's best friend. They travel the world together looking for exclusive stories. Susie wants to be ready for anything and everything, so she never travels anywhere without her equipment bag.

SUSIE'S EQUPIMENT BAG

Susie's bag is enormouse! It has lots of hidden, zipped compartments. Each pocket holds a different item, such as a camera, pliers, scissors, energy bars, a toothbrush, etc. The bag also has many special features. It can become a rucksack, a parachute, or an umbrella! And it's made of very lightweight but durable waterproof material.

"Listen to me, Geronimo," Susie squeaked "You should put a story about the Amazon on the front page. We have to do something to keep these rats from destroying the rainforest! I risked my fur to take these photos. Now the least you can do is publish them!"

"Nice work, Susie," I said proudly. "I can already see the headline: AMAZON RAINFOREST IN DANGER FROM –"

Before I could finish, my office door flew open and my cousin Trap burst in. He also works for the newspaper, though you'd never know it! He only shows up in the office when it's convenient for him. Anyway, he was pinching his nose with one

Pee-yew!

10

paw, and he held an umbrella in his other paw.

A letter dangled by a string from the tip of the umbrella. And as if that wasn't weird enough, a **cloud of flies** buzzed around the letter!

"You've got a letter, Geronimo!" Trap squeaked. "And boy, does it stink!"

He snipped the string with a pair of scissors and the letter landed on my desk with a flutter.

"Yuck, yuck, yuck!" Trap screeched. "Rat-munching rattlesnakes, where's this thing from? A landfill site? A sewage treatment plant? An underground cave full of rancid roaches that haven't bathed in years?"

He turned to leave, calling over his shoulder:

"You'd better close the door before you open that thing, Cuz! Everyone in the newsroom is complaining about the awful stench!"

I sighed. Was it my fault someone had sent me the

BANG!

SUSIE CLOSED THE DOOR

12

stinkiest letter in all of New Mouse City?!

A second later, Susie closed the door with a **BANG!**

Then she dashed to the window and threw it open. A gust of wind blew into the office, making it much easier to breathe.

Next she took a pair of tweezers out of her giant equipment bag. She *carefully* picked up the envelope.

Finally, she pulled out a magnifying glass and used it to examine the foul letter.

"That's odd," Susie remarked. "This comes

THEN SHE THREW OPEN THE WINDOW

SHE PICKED UP THE LETTER WITH A PAIR OF TWEEZERS ...

... AND EXAMINED IT CAREFULLY.

from Easter Island. Who would write to you from there, Geronimo?"

I shook my head in surprise.

"Musty Muenster, I have no idea!" I exclaimed. "Easter Island is one of the most **mysterious** places in the world ... and it's in the middle of nowhere!"

My paws trembled with excitement as I opened that strange, stinky envelope. Another surprise awaited me inside ... **The letter was from my sister Thea!**

Geronimo Stilton,
The Rodent's Gazette,
17 Swiss Cheese Centre,
New Mouse City,
Mouse Island, 13131

Dear Geronimo,

I've found a map that leads to treasure on Easter Island, and I've decided to search for it! I'm on the island right now. But I'm afraid finding the treasure could be very difficult, so that's why I'm sending you a copy of the map. If you receive this letter before I'm able to call you, it's because I may be in danger and I need your help. Find me by following the directions on the map. See you soon!

Love, Thea

P.S. Don't dilly-dally. Leave immediately!

P.P.S. Invite someone adventurous to come with you - someone like Wild Willie!

P.P.P.S. Take Susie with you as well. She can take photos to go along with my story, and The Rodent's Gazette will have the scoop of the year!

Furthermore, remember to update your will before leaving. This island is very mysterious, and who knows what might happen on a search for treasure. You may be leaving your fur behind!

One last thing: I hope you didn't find this letter too stinky. I wanted to keep any sneaky rodents from opening it and reading the map, so I dipped this letter in guano (that's bird poo, in case you were wondering). It stinks so much no one would ever want to open it! Aren't you impressed with my ingenuity?

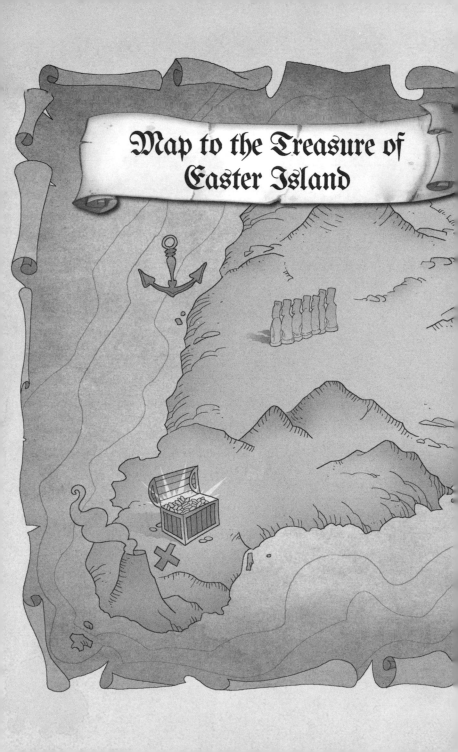

Find the biggest ahu and its fifteen protectors.
Turn west and search for the Great Water that is and isn't.
At the end of the day, follow the sun and you'll find the Seven Young Explorers.
Take seven gigantic steps to the right, three warrior steps to the left, and one baby step forwards.
The Sigh of the Wind will take you far away to the Big Black Bubble. There, the sea hides an ancient secret ...

THE TREASURE OF EASTER ISLAND!

Treasure, Treasure, Treasure!

"Wh-wh-what?" I stammered. "A map? Treasure? Easter Island?"

My whiskers trembled with fear. I didn't want to go on a treasure hunt! In case you didn't know it, I'm a real **SCAREDY-MOUSE.**

As soon as I uttered the word treasure, the door flew open and smacked me in the snout.

"Ouchie!" I squeaked.

It was my cousin Trap. He had clearly been standing just on the other side of the door, eavesdropping. He didn't even apologise.

"Treasure?" he squeaked, rubbing his paws together greedily. "I'm coming with you. Oh, what a beautiful word: treasure, treasure, treasure!"

"Trap, don't you understand?" I scolded him.

"The treasure isn't important – Thea is! I received her letter, but she hasn't called. That means she's in danger!"

Susie tried to call Thea on the phone, but she didn't answer at home or on her mobile.

"RAT-MUNCHING RATTLESNAKES!" I squeaked. "Thea must be in real danger! She always answers her mobile."

I was so worried about my sister that I fainted from fear. As I said, I'm a real scaredy-mouse.

But Susie managed to revive me. First, she smacked my cheek. ❶ Then she pinched my ear. ❷ Next she poured **ice-cold water** from a vase of flowers over my snout. ❸ Finally, she stuffed a piece of cheese into my mouth. ❹

While I was trying to get myself together, Susie called Wild Willie. Do you know him? He is an archaeologist and a true adventure mouse!

"Wild Willie, is that you?" Susie squeaked. "It's Susie, the official photographer for The Rodent's Gazette. Thea has disappeared … There's a treasure map … Easter Island … Right. We'll leave right away … Yeah, yeah … Won't dilly-dally … Right, right, right."

❶ Smack!

❷ Pinch!

❸ Splash!

❹ Eat!

20

Wild Willie?

She hung up.

"Wild Willie is on his way," she squeaked with satisfaction. "We're leaving immediately."

"Wh-what do you mean?" I stammered. "We're leaving right now? But I have to pack a bag! And turn on my out-of-office message! And say goodbye to my sweet nephew Benjamin!"

Suddenly, a gust of wind hit me right in the snout. Then I heard an incredible noise from outside my window.

Before I knew what was happening, a giant hook seemed to come out of the sky. A second later, I was dangling by my jacket collar as the hook scooped me up and carried me away!

"Heeeelp!" I squeaked.

I turned towards Trap and Susie, hoping they'd pull me inside. But instead, Trap grabbed my tail, and Susie grabbed his.

"Go with the adventure!" Susie shouted with a giggle as the hook lifted the three of us into the air.

MOULDY MOZZARELLA!

Where were we going?!

Heeeelp!

I'M ALIVE!
I'M STILL ALIVE!

A midnight-blue aeroplane with a fierce dragon painted on it flew overhead as we soared over the roofs of New Mouse City.

My whiskers quivered with fright. Have I mentioned that I get AIRSICK? And that's when I'm actually inside an aeroplane, not dangling below one!

"Heeeeeeeeeeeeelp!" I shrieked.

With a metallic screech, the cable above me began moving upwards. Finally, I landed inside the plane: THUMP!

"This is fabumouse!" Trap shouted.

"Awesome!" Susie squeaked in agreement.

But there were no shouts of excitement from me! I kissed the floor of the plane as I cried with relief.

"I'm alive! I'm still alive!"

"Well, for now …" a deep voice muttered. It was Wild Willie!

He was the one flying the plane! He handed me a map.

"Instead of wasting your breath, help me figure out the route to Easter Island," he squeaked. "And then read this travel guidebook!"

I was about to protest, but he stared at me with his piercing eyes.

"Don't you want to find Thea?" Wild Willie asked.

"Come on! Help me with the map. And don't make any mistakes, or we'll have to make an emergency landing in the middle of a stormy ocean or on top of a craggy mountain peak ..."

Emergency landing?! I quickly agreed to help. But when I opened the map, what I saw gave me chills from the top of my head to the tip of my tail. **Easter Island was far away and in the middle of nowhere!** And when I read the travel guide, I realised there were many, many mysteries surrounding the island ...

EASTER ISLAND

PACIFIC OCEAN

TEREVAKA VOLCANO

PUKATIKEI VOLCANO

POIKE

AHU AKIVI

AHU TONGARIKI

HOTU-ITI

OROI

HANGA ROA

MATAVERI INTERNATIONAL AIRPORT

VAIHU

CHILEAN SEA

AHU VINAPU

ORONGO

RANO KAU VOLCANO

THAT'S EASTER ISLAND!

Is That It?
No Way!

We flew for hours and hours. Wild Willie kept his gaze fixed on the flight instruments. He never moved away from the controls.

I, on the other paw, couldn't take my eyes off the foam-topped blue waves **CHURNING** and **CRASHING** below us. The ocean seemed endless. According to my guidebook, the Polynesian people who had once explored the area navigated the ocean in simple outrigger canoes! **How terrifying!**

Susie took photo after photo.

"Does this plane do stunts?" she asked Wild Willie as she snapped a shot of him at the controls.

He raised his left eyebrow. "Obviously," he replied coolly.

"Pff! I doubt it," Trap muttered.

Ahhhhhh!

Heeeelp!

To prove himself, Wild Willie immediately leaned on the controls, sending the plane into a wild corkscrew.

"**Heeeeelp!**" I screeched.

"Is that it?" Trap scoffed. "No way! You can't do anything better?"

With a sudden lurch, the plane dove into a death-defying spiral.

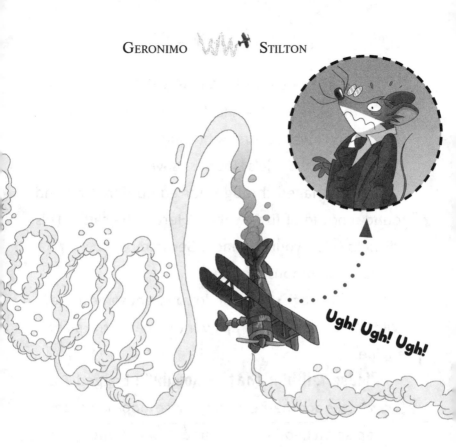

Ugh! Ugh! Ugh!

"Ahhhhhh!" I squeaked, terrified. **"I DON'T WANT TO LOSE MY FUR!"**

"Oh, that's nothing," Trap teased Willie. "If I were behind the controls ..."

Before Trap could finish his sentence, Wild Willie took the tiny plane through one breathtaking stunt after another.

33

During all these **DAREDEVIL MOVES**, I gripped the seat of the plane for dear life. My whiskers twisted with terror, and I was so airsick I thought I might lose my cheese! Luckily, Susie's kindness saved me.

She rummaged through her equipment bag and found a bottle of fizzy water. "Here," she said. "This will help settle your stomach, Geronimo."

Thank goodmouse for her!

"Is that enough stunts, or do you want some more?" Wild Willie shouted to Trap over the roar of the plane's engine.

"Please tell him that's enough!" I begged Trap. "I can't take another second of these loop-dee-loops!"

Trap scratched his snout and thought about it for what seemed like an eternity.

"Well, I have to admit those were some **PRETTY IMPRESSIVE STUNTS**," he conceded.

Only then did Wild Willie finally return the plane to a horizontal position. He grinned proudly.

A moment later, an island shaped like a triangle appeared on the horizon.

"We've arrived at Easter Island!" Susie squeaked excitedly.

"Yes, here we are, **in the middle of nowhere**," Wild Willie remarked darkly. "Did you remember to update your will, Geronimo?"

I shook my snout. When would I have had the time?

"Don't worry, Geronimo," Susie chirped. "I'll help you do it now. To whom would you like to leave The Rodent's Gazette?"

Trap tugged on my tail.

"Geronimo, my friend and favourite cousin," he said sweetly – a little too sweetly, if you ask me! "You're going to leave the paper to me, right? I know all about running a newspaper, unlike you. I think you should also leave me your antique cheese rind collection. And don't worry about your tombstone – I'll write something nice! How about: **Here lies Geronimo Stilton, a real scaredy-mouse! He met his end on Easter Island when he suffered an attack of uncontrollable fear.**"

That was something nice?!

"That's enough!" I squeaked. "Why does everyone

keep asking if I've updated my will, anyway?"

The three of them exchanged an understanding look. What were they keeping from me?

"He's a really jittery mouse, isn't he?" Wild Willie said.

"You're the ones who are making me jittery!" I said impatiently.

I put on my seat belt and closed my eyes. What kind of

danger awaited me? My heart beat faster just thinking about it. But my desire to help Thea was stronger than any fear I felt. I opened my wallet and took out a photo of my sister.

"I'll save you, little sister!" I whispered.

MY SISTER THEA STILTON

WELCOME TO RAPA NUI!

Before I knew it, the plane was landing at Mataveri International Airport. A friendly-looking rodent with **GOLDEN FUR** and long black hair met us at the gate.

"Welcome to Rapa Nui!" she greeted us. "My name is Vaitea, and I will be your guide."

Welcome!

She presented each of us with a garland of multicoloured flowers.

"We're not like other tourists," Trap boasted. I could tell he was trying to make a **good impression** on Vaitea. "We're here hunting for treas –"

Susie clapped her paw over Trap's snout before he could finish.

"Ahem, we're here on holiday, just like all these other tourists," Susie squeaked confidently. "We would love

39

to see the island's **most interesting** sights!"

Susie showed Vaitea a photo of Thea.

"This is our friend who was recently on the island," she said. "Have you ever seen her?"

"No, I'm sorry," Vaitea replied, shaking her head. "She doesn't look familiar."

We were all hungry from our long flight, so Vaitea took us to a great restaurant in the harbour. We ate huge grilled prawns, fish soup, and  **mahi mahi**, a fish that is often served on the island. During dinner, Vaitea told us some of the history of Easter Island.

MAHi MAHi

"Rapa Nui is the other name for Easter Island," she began. "It's also the name of the people who live here, and I'm proud to be one of them. My people speak two languages, Rapanui and Spanish."

Then she taught us a few words and phrases. I began taking notes: Rapanui was a very interesting language! At the end of dinner I showed off my knowledge and

SHORT DICTIONARY OF THE RAPANUI LANGUAGE

AHU: a structure or platform

HARE PA'ENGA: a traditional home that resembles an upside-down boat

IORANA: hello or goodbye; a greeting

MATU'A: ancestor, father

MOAI: a large statue

POKI: baby

RONGORONGO: wooden tablets with ancient carved writing

TOKI: a tool used to carve stone

TOTORA: a type of reed used to build rafts; a reed boat

VAI KAVA: ocean

Many inhabitants of Easter Island speak Rapanui, a Polynesian dialect. However, Chilean Spanish is the island's official language.

Rongorongo are ancient wooden tablets that feature carved symbols. These tablets have only been partially translated, so this written language is still a mystery!

said to Vaitea: "*Māuru-uru!* (Thank you!)"

"*Rivariva!* (Very good!)" Vaitea replied, smiling. "Now, would you like to see a typical dance?" she asked. "A performance is about to begin!"

The lights dimmed. Many young rodents appeared on the stage and began to sing. The musicians played ukuleles and drums, and a few people began to dance.

Their movements mimicked the daily activities of the Rapa Nui people, including swimming, fishing, and rowing a boat. Then they danced a ritual dance showing warriors intimidating their enemies. Finally, they concluded with a dance in which a fishermouse

and a maiden declared their love for each other. It was truly **fabumouse!**

Susie snapped a lot of photos.

"We'll leave here with lots of very interesting material for The Rodent's Gazette. Thea will be very happy with my work!"

Hearing Thea's name brought me back to reality. We were here on a mission!

Where was my sister Thea? And was she in danger? We had to find out soon.

Look for the Biggest Ahu ...

The next morning we gathered to decide what to do next. Wild Willie reread the riddle on the map:

FIND THE BIGGEST AHU AND ITS FIFTEEN PROTECTORS.

TURN WEST AND SEARCH FOR THE GREAT WATER THAT IS AND ISN'T.

AT THE END OF THE DAY, FOLLOW THE SUN AND YOU'LL FIND THE SEVEN YOUNG EXPLORERS.

TAKE SEVEN GIGANTIC STEPS TO THE RIGHT, THREE WARRIOR STEPS TO THE LEFT, AND ONE BABY STEP FORWARDS.

THE SIGH OF THE WIND WILL TAKE YOU FAR AWAY TO THE BIG BLACK BUBBLE.

THERE, THE SEA HIDES AN ANCIENT SECRET ...

THE TREASURE OF EASTER ISLAND!

"The first thing we need to do is to find an ahu," he

concluded. "In fact, we need to find the biggest one on the island."

I checked my Easter Island guidebook.

"The ahu are stone platforms that were used as *burial sites* by the ancient inhabitants of Easter Island," I explained.

At that moment, Vaitea came in.

"Perfect timing!" Susie squeaked. "We were just talking about where we'd like to go first. We'd like to see some of the island's ahu. Can you tell us which one is the biggest?"

"That would be Ahu Tongariki," Vaitea replied with a smile. "It's one of the most **spectacular** places on the island!"

Hmm, let's see ...

When we got to Ahu Tongariki, the most majestic sight awaited us.

The 𐤄NORMOVS𐤄 statues lined the shore, their backs to the ocean waves. Vaitea explained that the statues – called moai – were built to guard and protect the island.

"Get your camera ready, Susie!" Trap shouted as he ran towards a moai. "I'm going to climb to the top."

"Stop!" Vaitea squeaked in dismay. "You can't climb a moai! Please, you shouldn't even touch it! This is my ancestors' sacred burial ground."

AHU TONGARIKI

Ahu Tongariki is the biggest ahu on Easter Island. The moai there face inland with their backs to the sea.

Susie grabbed Trap by the tail a second before he began to climb.

"WHAT DO YOU THINK YOU'RE DOING?!" she scolded him.

During this whole mess, I was busy counting the moai on the stone platforms.

"One, two, three, four, five ... thirteen, fourteen, fifteen!" I counted. "These are the fifteen protectors the riddle talks about. We figured out the first clue!"

They're amazing!

"Now we have to turn west and find the Great Water," whispered Wild Willie. "But I don't understand why it 'is and isn't'. **What do you think that means?"**

STOP! Paws off! Argh!

SEARCHING FOR THE GREAT WATER

We headed west with Vaitea, but we didn't see even **A DROP OF WATER** anywhere!

"Is there any water on Easter Island?" Susie asked her. "I haven't seen any so far."

"Well, there is and isn't much water on the island," Vaitea replied mysteriously. "There are three crater lakes. But during the dry season, there isn't much water in them. During the rainy season, though, it's another story ..."

My tail twisted with excitement. Vaitea had referred to water that "is and isn't"!

"Is one of these crater lakes near here?" I asked eagerly.

She nodded and motioned for us to follow her up a steep path. We turned a corner, and there before us

was a rocky crater etched deep into the ground.

**"This is where the Great Water flows ...
when there is any!"**

This is where the Great Water flows?

Seven Young Explorers

Wild Willie smiled with satisfaction and immediately checked the map.

"The map says, 'At the end of the day, follow the sun,'" he said. "So we should head west, since that's where the sun sets."

I scratched my head.

"Yes, but what are the Seven Young Explorers?"

We got back in Vaitea's car and headed towards the western shore of the island. As we mused over the riddle, we were as quiet as mice.

Night had already fallen, and Vaitea stared at the dark sky. A **silvery moon** shone brightly.

"In the olden days, it was precisely on nights like these that our ancestors performed sacred ceremonies near the moai by the sea," she told us. "Those ceremonies

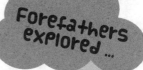

Moa by the sea ...

Polynesia ...

Forefathers explored ...

Ancient traditions ...

Sacred ceremonies ...

recalled the ancient traditions of Polynesia, which is where my courageous forefathers came from when they explored this new land."

It all sounded very, very familiar. But where had I heard it before?

Vaitea's words kept turning over and over in my head. Then suddenly it was like a **light bulb** turned on. I had read those words before in my travel guide! I leafed through it until I found what I was looking for.

"Listen to this!" I told the others, reading from the book. "'Most of the moai on Easter Island look inwards with their backs to the sea. But there is one group of seven moai that look towards the sea.'" I turned towards

52

Listen to this! Vaitea eagerly. "Do you know where these seven moai are?"

"Of course," she replied immediately. "They are at Ahu Akivi. I can take you there right now if you wish. They represent the **seven young explorers** who left Polynesia to look for new land, and finally reached Easter Island."

Susie, Trap, Wild Willie, and I exchanged a look. We had solved the next clue!

Vaitea turned the car onto a long dirt road full of potholes. Then we came to a stop in a clearing. We quickly climbed out, eager with excitement. The four of us ran towards the summit of the small hill. At the top of the hill was a platform with seven moai standing in a row. The full moon bathed them with a silvery light, surrounding them with a halo of mystery.

"These must be the Seven Young Explorers!" I whispered to Susie.

AHU AKIVI

Ahu Akivi is found inland instead of along the coast like the other ahu on Easter Island. It is also the only site where the moai look out towards the ocean.

THE SIGH OF THE WIND

Vaitea noticed me and Susie whispering, and she studied us closely with her bright eyes.

"Excuse me, I don't mean to be **RUDE**, but I don't think you've told me the truth about why you are here," she began. "I have a feeling you're not simply tourists."

I looked at my friends. I was more than happy to tell Vaitea the truth, but I wasn't sure what they were thinking.

Susie smiled. "It's okay with me if we tell her," she said. "I trust Vaitea."

Wild Willie nodded. "Me too."

"**Hmpf!**" Trap squeaked. "Well, I don't want to tell her. I don't want to share the treasure with anyone!"

Susie gave Trap a stern look. "Aren't you **ASHAMED** of being so greedy?" she asked. "We're searching for Thea, not the treasure!"

"You might be searching for Thea, but I'm looking for the **treasure**," Trap admitted with a shrug. **He didn't seem ASHAMED at all!**

The two of them began squabbling. Wild Willie had to pull them apart!

"Three to one," Willie told Trap. "The majority wins. Geronimo, explain everything to Vaitea!"

"My sister Thea came here in search of treasure, but she's gone **MISSING**!" I told Vaitea. "She never returned home to New Mouse City. So now we're looking for the same treasure in the hope of finding her!"

Vaitea thought it over.

"I'll help!" she offered.

Meanwhile, Trap was busy following the directions on the map. He had run in front of the seven moai and began counting in a loud voice.

"Okay," he squeaked. "The map says to take seven gigantic steps to the right, three warrior steps to the left, and one baby step forwards ..."

He had just taken the baby step when his paw landed on something that looked like a plain old rock. But it wasn't a rock. **It was a hole!**

With a yelp, Trap fell into it – down, down, down!

We ran towards the hole, but it was too late. My cousin had **disappeared!**

SEVEN GIGANTIC STEPS TO THE RIGHT ...

THREE WARRIOR STEPS TO THE LEFT ...

Wild Willie twirled his whiskers thoughtfully.

"The riddle did say, '**THE SIGH OF THE WIND** will take you far away,'" he said.

"We've got to do something!" Susie squeaked.

"Are you ready for an adventure?" Wild Willie shouted. "If you are, follow me!"

He held out his paw to Susie, who held out her paw to me. In turn, I held out my paw to Vaitea. A moment later, Wild Willie jumped into the hole, taking the rest of us with him!

MOULDY MOZZARELLA! How do I get myself into these messes?!

ONE BABY STEP FORWARDS ...

HELP!

THE BIG BLACK BUBBLE

We found ourselves inside a damp, dark underground tunnel. I was terrified! I couldn't see a whisker!

What's more, there was a continuous rustling noise, as if a gigantic creature was lying there, breathing in the dark. I let out **A SHRIEK OF TERROR** as we plummeted deeper and deeper into the underground passageway. We seemed to be travelling to the centre of the Earth. A moment later, I was no longer sliding down the tunnel – I was floating in the air! *THE SIGH OF THE WIND* was carrying us along!

We floated along in the tunnel for a long time. Then instead of descending further, we began to rise until the wind finally deposited us on firm ground. Trap had already emerged and was rubbing his bruised tail. Wild Willie bounded out, but his hat remained floating in mid-air as if on top of an invisible fountain. Willie

grabbed it quickly and put it back on his head.

I glanced around me and made sure everyone was okay.

"Trap, Susie, Wild Willie, Vaitea, and me!" I squeaked. "All here!"

I breathed a sigh of relief. Then I looked around, taking in my surroundings.

We found ourselves inside an enormouse cave with a rounded ceiling. It looked like a big, dark bubble. There was a saltwater lagoon in the middle of the cave. I gently touched the wall: it was dark, porous volcanic rock.

"THE BIG BLACK BUBBLE!" whispered Susie. "We found it!"

WHERE ARE WE GOING?

Argh!

"This is where the **treasure** is!" Trap squeaked with excitement.

Susie turned to him, an angry look on her snout.

"No, this is where we might find Thea!" she corrected him. "How can you only think of the **treasure**? You should be **ASHAMED** of yourself!"

Meanwhile, Wild Willie examined the map.

"I checked the direction on the compass while we were travelling on *THE SIGH OF THE WIND*," he whispered. "We travelled underground in a south-west direction."

"That means we're now right under the Rano Kau

Ahhh!

Help!

crater!" Vaitea added. "We're in the heart of a volcano. And this must be a **secret** underground lagoon. I've never seen it on any map, and I've been a guide on this island since I was a tiny mouselet!"

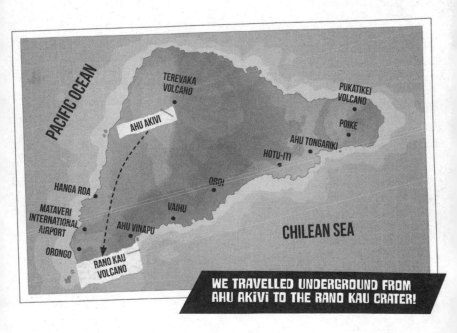

WE TRAVELLED UNDERGROUND FROM
AHU AKIVI TO THE RANO KAU CRATER!

PIRATES IN THE NIGHT

As they were talking, Susie snapped some photos of Wild Willie checking the map. The camera's flash lit the rocks behind us.

At the same time, Trap sneezed. The sound bounced off the surrounding walls, **ECHOING** loudly.

ACHOO! CHOO! CHOO! CHOO!

A second later we heard a squeak. We weren't alone in the cave! And the *FLASH* of the camera and the echo of the sneeze had revealed our presence to whoever else was there.

Wild Willie motioned to us to keep quiet. Then he scampered behind some rocks and squatted down. We immediately followed his example. A moment later, we heard an unfriendly voice.

"Search there, at the end of the cave," the voice commanded. **"And if you find anyone, bring them to me!"**

"Maybe somebody came looking for that nosy little mouse and the professor," another voice replied.

I shivered. Was "that nosy mouse" my sister Thea? But who was the professor?

"Let's get back to the ship!" the first voice yelled. "We have to finish loading the treasure. We'll leave tonight!"

"Yes, Captain," the other rodent replied. "But what are we going do with our prisoners? They know everything. We can't leave them here!"

My whiskers trembled with fear.

"I'll figure it out later," grumbled the captain. "Now let's go! Get the prisoners and bring them to the ship. They may still be useful!"

Someone was coming
towards us, but Wild Willie
signalled to us to follow him quietly.

Afraid of being seen, we slithered across
the cave floor on our elbows until we reached
the shore of the lagoon, where we saw a **GIANT**
pirate ship!

The ship had a slim shape and a huge sail to better
cruise the waves. It was completely black – including
the sails – and I could see its name on the side:
PHANTOM OF THE NIGHT.

Susie pointed to something hanging from the
tip of a rock

high above us. **IT WAS A GIANT CAGE!** Inside was my sister Thea and Professor von Dustyfur, a famous archaeologist who specialises in **ancient treasures**.

The short, round pirate moved towards the cage. I was about to run over to save my sister and the professor when Wild Willie grabbed me by the tail.

"Wait!" he whispered. "Just be quiet. Let's see what happens."

The pirate lowered the cage using a pulley. Then he opened it, nudged my sister and the professor out of the cage, and tied their paws behind their backs. He left them behind a giant pile of crates.

"DON'T MOVE, GOT IT?" he hissed. "The captain hasn't decided what to do with you yet!"

The other pirates loaded the crates onto the ship one at a time, arranging them neatly in the cargo compartment. As the pirates worked, the captain barked insults at his crew.

"Hurry up or I'll feed you to the sharks for dinner!" he squeaked menacingly.

Soon all the pirates had disappeared inside the ship, leaving Thea and the professor alone. I signalled to the others, and we crept quickly but quietly to their side.

"Shhh! Thea, it's me, Geronimo!" I whispered. **"We came to save you!"**

Argh!

PRISONERS, COME TO ME!

The Treasure of Rapa Nui

Thea's eyes lit up when she saw me. Luckily, she and the professor remained silent. I picked up a sharp sliver of rock and used it to saw through the ropes that bound their paws.

"Follow me," I whispered to them. "But don't make a sound!"

The pirates were busy preparing for their departure, so they didn't see us sneak away from the ship. We slipped behind some rocks out of the pirates' view.

"Thank you, Geronimo!" Thea said, hugging me affectionately. "I knew you'd come to save me!"

Professor von Dustyfur also thanked me warmly. I introduced Susie, Trap, Wild Willie, and Vaitea.

"I would never have been able to find you without their help," I told Thea and the professor.

"What are these pirates up to?" Willie asked, pointing to the ship.

"Well, I came to the island and followed the instructions on the map, just like you," Thea explained. "First I found the largest ahu with the fifteen moai, then the **GREAT WATER**, then the **Seven Young Explorers**, and finally the **BIG BLACK BUBBLE**."

The rest of us leaned in, eager to hear what happened next.

"Here, under the **BIG BLACK BUBBLE**, I found the real treasure of Rapa Nui. But unfortunately, I also found these pirates, and I was captured. That's when I met the professor. He was the pirates' hostage!"

The professor sighed. "It's true," he explained. "They forced me to unearth many ancient treasures for them."

"Bingo!" Trap squeaked with excitement. "Tell us about the treasure of Rapa Nui. Is it a chest of gold coins? Or a heap of precious stones and pearls?"

Thea's Adventure

1

Thea arrived on Easter Island and searched for the precious treasure by following the directions on the map.

2

She entered the Tunnel of the Sigh of the Wind ...

3

She came to the Big Black Bubble ...

4

... and she was captured by pirates! That's when she met the professor, who had been their prisoner for many months.

Susie elbowed him sharply.

But Thea knew our cousin Trap too well. She just smiled at him.

"Cousin, the treasure I found in this cave is very precious, but you won't be taking it home to New Mouse Island with you," she said simply. "This treasure is for the inhabitants of Easter Island!"

"But what is it?" Trap squeaked.

Thea pointed to seven canoes woven from reeds. They had been hidden in a corner of the cave.

This is the treasure of Rapa Nui!

That's it?

"What are those?" Trap asked.

"This is the treasure of Rapa Nui!" Thea said, gesturing to the seven small boats. "These are the seven ancient canoes that the **seven courageous young explorers** used to travel to Easter Island from Polynesia," she explained.

"Oooohh ... That's it?" Trap moaned, his whiskers **drooping** with disappointment.

"Yes," Thea said with a smile. "I was searching for the seven ancient canoes. But the pirates were looking for another treasure – one they found by forcing the professor to help them! Now they're loading it onto their ship ... Come on, I'll show you!"

We followed Thea to a **HUGE** block covered with a cloth on the shore of the lagoon.

"This treasure was found at the bottom of the sea," Thea whispered.

She lifted a corner of the cloth to reveal a bright, **shining** surface. It was a moai made of solid gold!

"NOW, THIS IS WHAT I CALL A TREASURE!" Trap squeaked, licking his whiskers greedily. "Let's see now. I only need a teeny-tiny piece of this statue and I'll be rich! Why don't I just chip off a little sliver ..."

Susie pinched his ear.

"Don't you dare touch it!" she warned,

Wild Willie looked at him sternly.

"The moai are sacred here in Rapa Nui," he said

Come and look!

Wow!

seriously. "Those pirates will soon regret taking a treasure that does not belong to them."

"Okay, okay," Trap sulked. **"I was only kidding!"**

I only need a teeny-tiny piece ...

Don't you dare!

THE SEVEN CANOES

We barely had time to cover up the treasure again before we heard the captain bark, **"LOAD THE MOAI!"** to the pirates.

A giant crane descended from the ship's deck, grabbing the gold moai and lifting it up onto the ship.

Thea desperately turned to Wild Willie.

"What can we do?" she asked.

"We have to take action!" he replied. "Let's get out of here, fast, and look for help!"

Vaitea turned towards the tunnel we had entered from.

"We can't leave that way," she said. "The wind only blows in this direction!"

Wild Willie smiled.

"We'll leave by sea ... in the seven canoes!"

Follow me!

Luckily, the cool temperature in the tunnel had preserved the canoes over time. They were in **perfect** condition, and very fast! We began to paddle, careful not to make a sound.

As we got closer and closer to the ship, I was so scared the pirates might see us. My whiskers trembled with fright! Luckily, the pirates were too busy moving the moai. They didn't notice us slip by silently in the dark water. We paddled around the ship and headed to the mouth of the cave. When we finally emerged into the open sea, we found ourselves under a starry night sky that was lit up by the **silvery light of the moon**.

We saw a small beach nearby. Wild Willie was first to set his paw on land.

"Let's quickly gather some dry wood," he said. "We'll light a big fire and then I'll make some signals that will attract the attention of mice all the way in the village!"

While we threw more wood on the fire, Wild Willie used a blanket to create smoke signals. He used Morse code to send a distress signal: **SOS**.

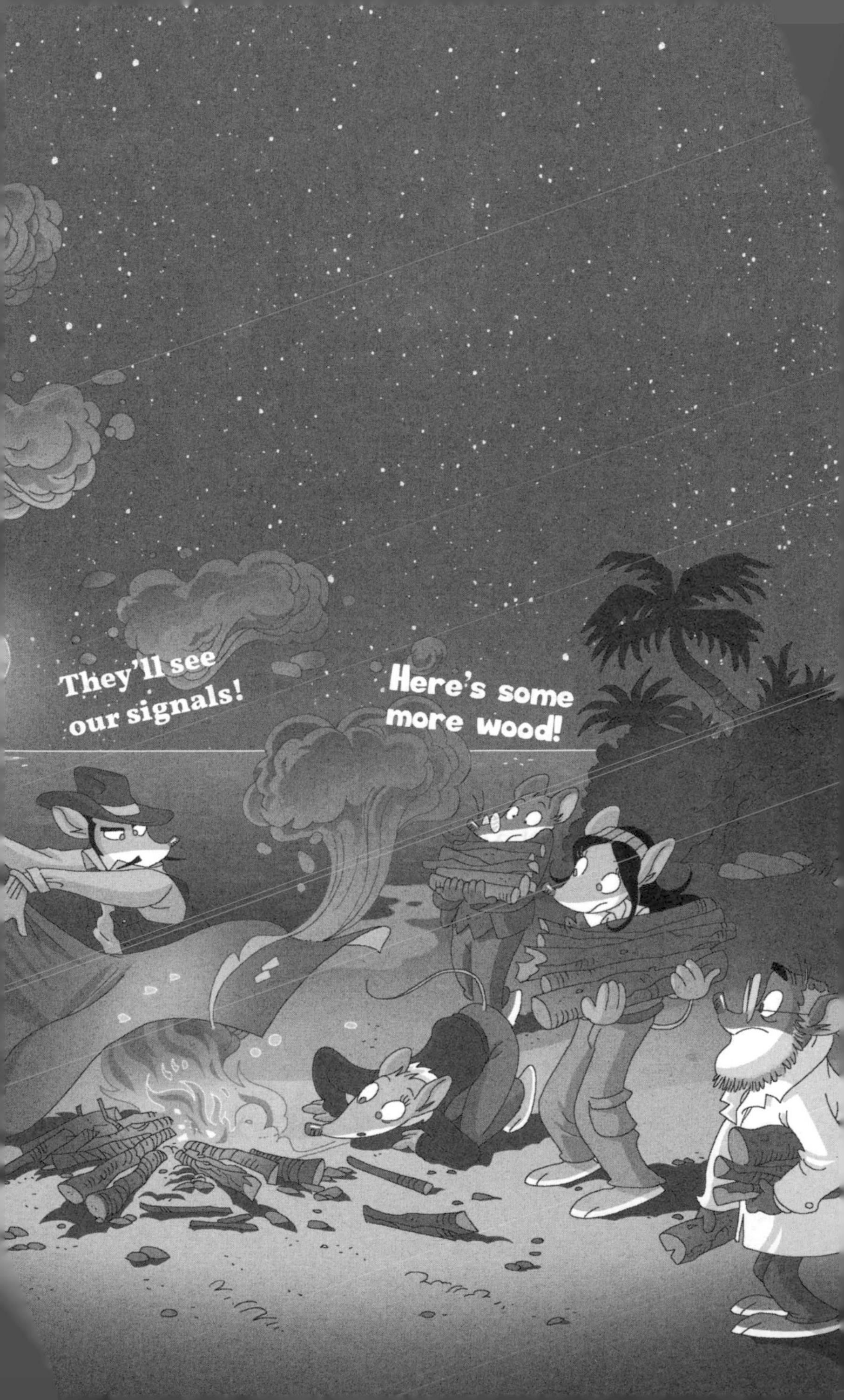
They'll see our signals!
Here's some more wood!

Suddenly we saw the bow of the PHANTOM OF THE NIGHT emerge from the secret cave. The pirates' ship was weighed down heavily with the gold moai. Unfortunately for us, they spotted our fire right away. The pirates pointed their cannons in our direction, and we could hear the captain issue his command.

"Shoot those spies!" the captain growled. "Ready! Aim! Fire!"

"Help!" I squeaked. "They'll flatten us into mouse pancakes!"

I closed my eyes and waited for the cannonball to squash us, but nothing happened! I slowly opened one eye and then the other, and saw why. The pirates' ship was SINKING from the weight of the gold moai!

MORSE CODE

Morse code is a communication system invented by Samuel Morse, an American painter and inventor. The code translates numbers and letters of the alphabet into a series of signals of different duration - either short dots or long dashes. The help signal, SOS, in Morse code is very simple: three short dots, three long dashes, and three short dots.

Wild Willie chuckled.

"I knew those pirates would be sorry they stole that!" he said.

A moment later, a helicopter appeared in the night sky, dozens of boats sailed over the horizon and headed towards our beach, and cars and trucks sped towards us over land. **Everyone had seen our SOS and had come to our aid!**

And as for the pirates who had been shipwrecked in the middle of the bay – well, they wouldn't be getting away.

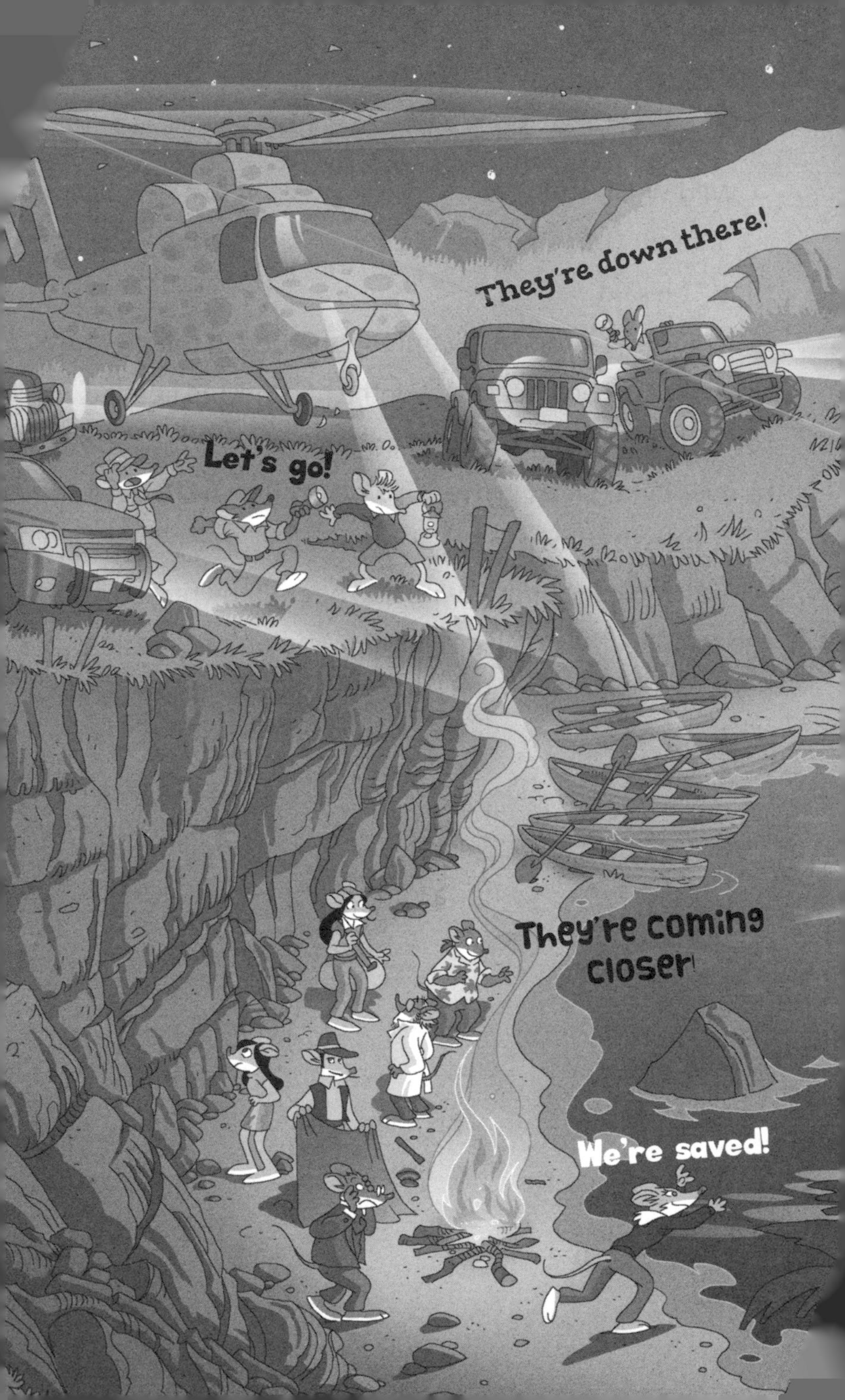

They're down there!
Let's go!
They're coming closer!
We're saved!

GOODBYE!

We gave the seven canoes to the inhabitants of Easter Island. They were so happy to be reunited with such a **precious** historical treasure – one that had led to the discovery of Rapa Nui!

To thank us, they organised an amazing party for us on the beach. They sang and danced for us and put flower garlands around our necks.

"What will you do about the gold moai?" Trap asked Vaitea during the party. "Are you going to fish it out of the water?"

Vaitea shook her head. "It's resting in the sea again," she replied. "And that's where it's going to stay!"

Soon it was time for us to say **goodbye**. We climbed into Vaitea's car and headed to the airport, the sounds of the Polynesian music and the blue sea fading behind us.

"Thank you for returning the treasure to the Rapa Nui people," Vaitea told us.

"No, thank you!" I replied. **"We couldn't have done it without your help!"**

We waved goodbye as we boarded Wild Willie's plane.

Wild Willie settled into his pilot's seat.

"Captain here," he said to himself with a smile. "We're leaving Easter Island. In a few hours we'll be flying over the coast of Chile. Our trip will continue all the way home to **Mouse Island**!"

Suddenly, I realised that our incredible adventure had come to an end. We were going home!

I thought of all my friends waiting for me and for Thea back in New Mouse City. I was especially looking

Goodbye, Rapa Nui!

forward to seeing my adorable nephew Benjamin. As I thought of my loved ones on Mouse Island, I looked out of the window of the plane. The triangular outline of Easter Island, which was wrapped in a mass of clouds, receded into the distance.

"Goodbye, Rapa Nui!" I whispered softly under my whiskers.

SPECIAL EDITION OF THE RODENT'S GAZETTE!

As soon as we landed at New Mouse City's airport, I hurried to the office of The Rodent's Gazette.

"Hello!" I greeted the staff. "I'm back from Easter Island, and I need everyone's help to put out an extra-special edition of the paper!"

The entire staff pitched in, and in just a few hours, we had put together an **amazing** special edition of The Rodent's Gazette. It included notes from Thea's diary and Susie's incredible photographs. That evening, the paper went on sale. It was a **fabumouse** success!

Everyone had worked so hard on the newspaper, and I was hoping my grandfather William Shortpaws would be pleased. But all he did was pinch my ear.

"I have to admit that this time you did a pretty good job, Grandson," he barked. "But don't get comfortable!

I've got my eye on you all the time, got it?"

I just rolled my eyes at him.

Night fell and I headed home at last. As I walked down the streets of New Mouse City, I met rodents around every corner.

They greeted me with hugs and smiles and asked me lots of questions about my adventure.

"It's nice to have you back here in New Mouse City. We missed you!"

I was so happy to be surrounded by so many friends and neighbours who loved me.

The Rodent's Gazette
The most famouse newspaper on Mouse Island

THE TREASURE OF EASTER ISLAND FOUND!

NEW MOUSE CITY— Special correspondent Thea Stilton of The Rodent's Gazette and Professor von Dustyfur, the noted archaeologist and expert in ancient treasures, have returned home to Mouse Island after being abducted by pirates. The famouse journalist had gone to Easter Island in search of the lost treasure.

There, she was captured by a band of ruthless pirates who had been holding Professor von Dustyfur captive … (continued)

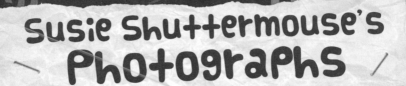

Trap stuffing his snout with shrimp!

GERONIMO ENCOUNTERS A MYSTERIOUS MOAI

The joy of dance!

DON'T TOUCH THE MOAI, TRAP!

GERONIMO ABOUT TO THROW UP

Thea and the professor: the pirates' prisoners

THE SEVEN CANOES: THE REAL TREASURE OF RAPA NUI!

FINALLY HOME ... OR MAYBE NOT?

I finally arrived home, feeling **exhausted**. With a sigh of relief, I put on my pyjamas, made myself a nice cup of hot tea, and slipped beneath the covers of my comfy bed. It felt so good to be back!

Then the telephone **RANG**.

"Hello?" I answered. "Stilton here. *Geronimo Stilton!*"

I heard Susie's familiar squeak.

"Hi, Geronimo!" she chirped brightly. "I really liked travelling with you."

Then I heard Thea's voice in the background.

"Tell him he's coming with us on our next trip!" she squeaked.

"That's right," Susie said. "We have another mystery to solve – and we're going to **MACHU PICCHU** in Peru!"

"Don't worry, Cuz, I'm coming, too!" shouted Trap. I guess he was also there. "Aren't you thrilled? Now pack your little things and we'll come by to pick you up soon!"

"That's right, **CHEESEHEAD**!" Wild Willie chimed in. "Get ready for an adventure!"

"N-no!" I stammered. "That is, thanks a million, but I'm not ready. I mean, I'd love to come, but I have too much work to catch up on. So, no, thanks! Have a nice trip. Goodbye!"

I heard a chorus of confused protests at the other end of the phone. But then Wild Willie's deep voice cut them off.

"If we say you're coming,

Are you ready for an adventure?

you're coming," he squeaked. "Period!"

"Got it, Cuz?" Trap shouted. "Period! That means no excuses!"

"You'll see, Geronimo!" Thea added. "You're actually very ready for the **next adventure**!"

"No, no, no!" I replied. "I'm telling you I'm not ready at all!"

But unfortunately they had already hung up the phone.

I stayed in bed and thought about it for a while as my whiskers quivered with uncertainty. But then my eyes fell on a photo of the five of us on Easter Island. I looked happy in it, and I hate to admit it, but ... I almost looked like an **ADVENTUROUS** mouse! I sighed and looked out the window to the landscape of New Mouse City.

It was a familiar view, and one that I knew well: there was Singing Stone Plaza, and the Fashion District, and the harbour with its bobbing sailboats ...

Yes, it was great being home. But it had also

been great going on an **amazing** adventure far, far away. When you're travelling, everything is a challenge and courage is greatly rewarded. I stared far off into the horizon. Suddenly I felt brave and confident.

"I *am* ready for a new adventure!" I exclaimed. "A whisker-licking good one!"

And I promise to tell you all about it in my next book. Rodent's honour!

Ah, sweet New Mouse City!

THE RODENT'S GAZETTE

1. Main entrance
2. Printing presses (where everything is printed)
3. Accounts department
4. Editorial room (where editors, illustrators, and designers work)
5. Geronimo Stilton's office
6. Geronimo's botanical garden

MAP OF New Mouse CITY

1. Industrial Zone
2. Cheese Factories
3. Angorat International Airport
4. WRAT Radio and Television Station
5. Cheese Market
6. Fish Market
7. Town Hall
8. Snotnose Castle
9. The Seven Hills of Mouse Island
10. Mouse Central Station
11. Trade Centre
12. Movie Theatre
13. Gym
14. Catnegic Hall
15. Singing Stone Plaza
16. The Gouda Theatre
17. Grand Hotel
18. Mouse General Hospital
19. Botanical Gardens
20. Cheap Junk for Less (Trap's store)
21. Parking Lot
22. Mouseum of Modern Art
23. University and Library
24. The Daily Rat
25. The Rodent's Gazette
26. Trap's House
27. Fashion District
28. The Mouse House Restaurant
29. Environmental Protection Centre
30. Harbour Office
31. Mousidon Square Garden
32. Golf Course
33. Swimming Pool
34. Blushing Meadow Tennis Courts
35. Curlyfur Island Amusement Park
36. Geronimo's House
37. Historic District
38. Public Library
39. Shipyard
40. Thea's House
41. New Mouse Harbour
42. Luna Lighthouse
43. The Statue of Liberty
44. Hercule Poirat's Office
45. Petunia Pretty Paws's House
46. Grandfather William's House

MAP OF MOUSE ISLAND

1. Big Ice Lake
2. Frozen Fur Peak
3. Slipperyslopes Glacier
4. Coldcreeps Peak
5. Ratzikistan
6. Transratania
7. Mount Vamp
8. Roastedrat Volcano
9. Brimstone Lake
10. Poopedcat Pass
11. Stinko Peak
12. Dark Forest
13. Vain Vampires Valley
14. Goosebumps Gorge
15. The Shadow Line Pass
16. Penny-Pincher Castle
17. Nature Reserve Park
18. Las Ratayas Marinas
19. Fossil Forest
20. Lake Lake
21. Lake Lakelake
22. Lake Lakelakelake
23. Cheddar Crag
24. Cannycat Castle
25. Valley of the
    Giant Sequoia
26. Cheddar Springs
27. Sulphurous Swamp
28. Old Reliable Geyser
29. Vole Vale
30. Ravingrat Ravine
31. Gnat Marshes
32. Munster Highlands
33. Mousehara Desert
34. Oasis of the
    Sweaty Camel
35. Cabbagehead Hill
36. Rattytrap Jungle
37. Rio Mosquito
38. Mousefort Beach
39. San Mouscisco
40. Swissville
41. Cheddarton
42. Mouseport
43. New Mouse City
44. Pirate Ship of Cats

THE COLLECTION

HAVE YOU READ ALL OF GERONIMO'S ADVENTURES?

ABOUT THE
AUTHOR

Born in New Mouse City, Mouse Island, GERONIMO STILTON is Rattus Emeritus of Mousomorphic Literature and of Neo-Ratonic Comparative Philosophy. For the past twenty years, he has been running The Rodent's Gazette, New Mouse City's most widely read daily newspaper.

Stilton was awarded the Ratitzer Prize for his scoops on *The Curse of the Cheese Pyramid* and *The Search for Sunken Treasure*. He has also received the Andersen Prize for Personality of the Year. His works have been published all over the globe.

In his spare time, Mr. Stilton collects antique cheese rinds and plays golf. But what he most enjoys is telling stories to his nephew Benjamin.